Monsters!

Monsters!

Monsters!

Monsters stomp

and stamp.

Monsters bash

and crash.

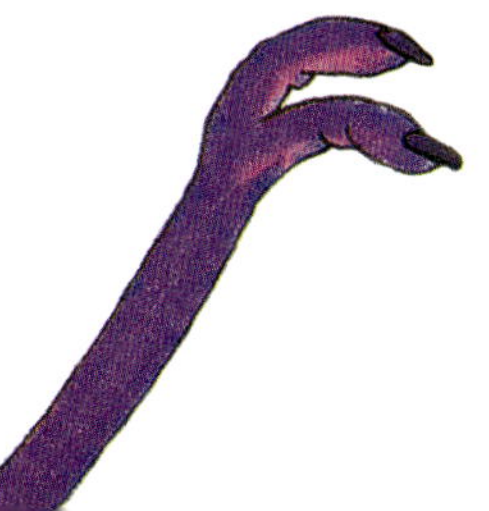

Monsters flap

and clap.

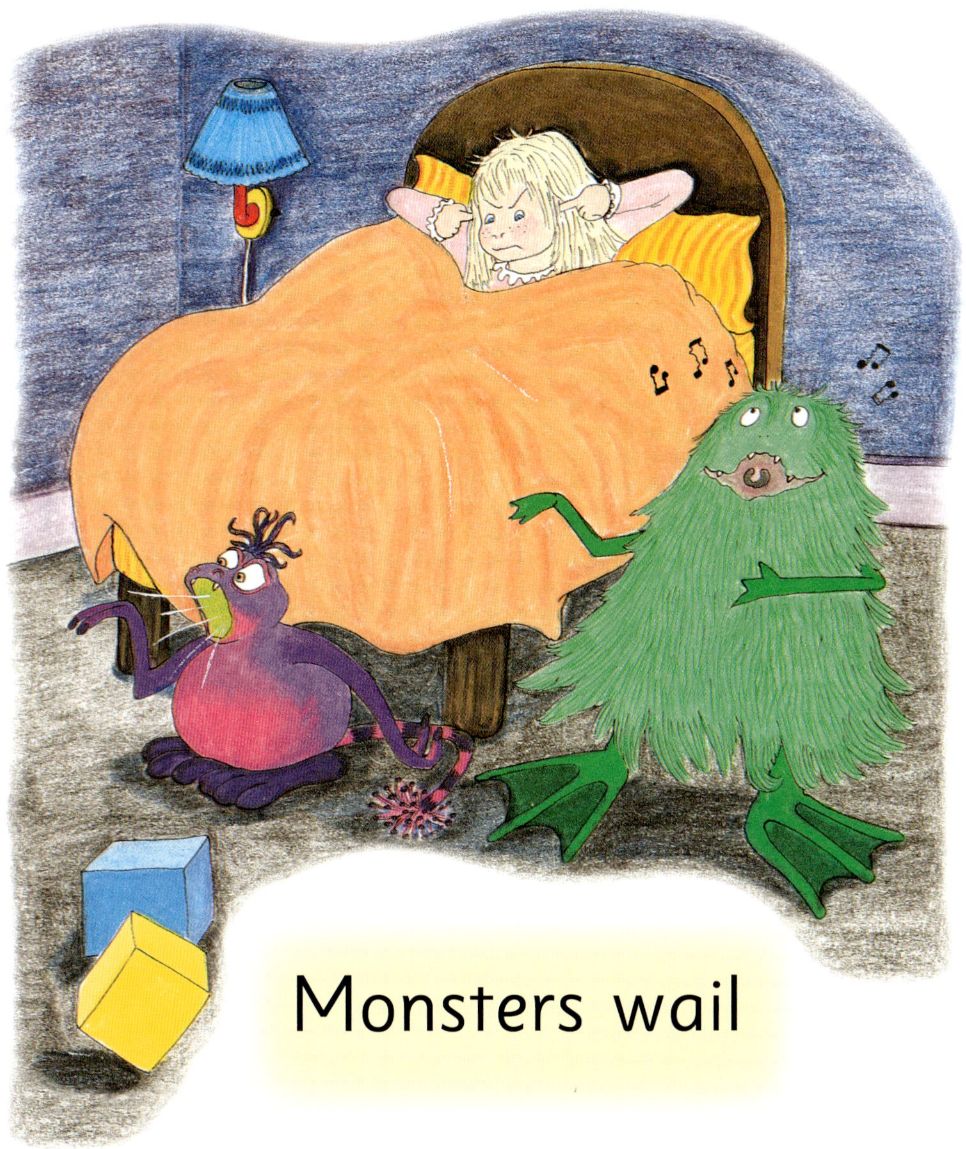

Monsters wail

and shout.

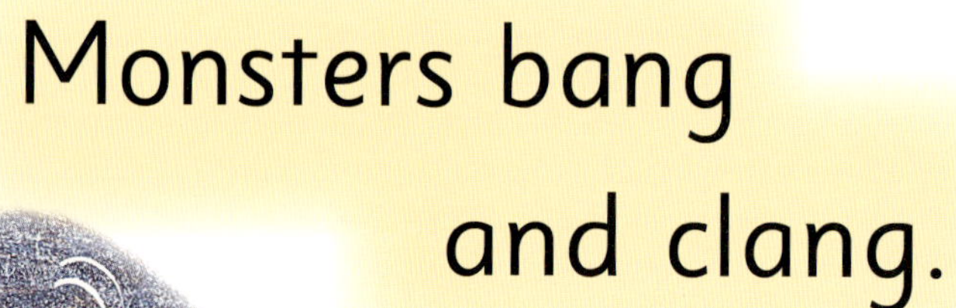

Monsters bang
and clang.

Monsters

hop, then stop!

Monsters are sleeping.

Sh!